Tom, Sid, the Goth and the Ghost

By Jenny Alexander
illustrated by Terry McKenna

Contents

PEARSON
Longman

Text © Jenny Alexander 2004
Series editors: Martin Coles and Christine Hall

PEARSON EDUCATION LIMITED
Edinburgh Gate
Harlow
Essex CM20 2JE
England

www.longman.co.uk

First published 2004
ISBN 0582 79628 8

Illustrated by Terry McKenna (Linda Rogers)

Printed in Great Britain by Scotprint, Haddington

The publishers' policy is to use paper manufactured from sustainable forests.

1 Tom, Sid ...

Tom, that's me. Thomas J Baxter, football superstar! Well, maybe that isn't one hundred per cent true, but everything else is. It's the one hundred per cent true story of what happened to me in the holidays.

Two days after the end of term the 'For Sale' sign outside our house got a big red 'SOLD' sticker across it. We had been looking for a smaller house for a few months, though I couldn't see why. Our house seemed to me to be just the right size, plus it had a big garden, plus it was near the park. Why would we want to buy a smaller one?

As it turned out, we were buying two smaller ones. Mum and Mel were going to have a flat near the middle of town, and Dad and I were getting a little terraced house in Miller's Row. I was pretty annoyed that no one had told me what was going on beforehand. It wasn't as if Mum and Dad had been at each other's throats for months, like my friend Luke's parents before they split up. It wasn't as if I could've seen it coming. One day everything seemed to be fine, and the next day there was Mum saying, "Things aren't working out, Dad and I are splitting up. We've already organised where we're going to live."

I stayed angry right through the packing; it got me through. Otherwise, I'd have been blubbing like a baby. It isn't easy putting all your stuff into boxes, and it's even worse seeing your mum and dad dividing everything else up.

When we got to the new house I was still angry. I made sure Dad knew I didn't like it. It was so pokey and small. Even with only half our furniture in it, it looked too full. There were only two rooms downstairs, and a kitchen built on at the back. By the time we'd got all the boxes in, the living room was full up.

Upstairs, there was a bedroom for Dad and a bathroom, plus my bedroom over the kitchen. It was a cold room with white walls, a bit grubby in places, dotted with bits of Blu-Tack where someone else's pictures had been. "It's not bad," Dad goes, trying to sound cheerful but not managing it. "You've got a good view of the garden."

The garden was a narrow strip, completely choked with stinging nettles and brambles. There was a shed at the end with a broken door, and lots of junk was spilling out. Bike wheels, bits of carpet, an old washing machine ... "It needs a bit of tidying up," Dad said.

He left me to unpack. I didn't want to. It felt like if we kept the stuff in the boxes we might still be able to change our minds and go back. I could hear Dad moving about downstairs.

There wasn't any murmur of TV noise or muffled beat of music, and everything sounded too loud in the silence. After a while he came up to see how I was getting on.

"It looks like you need a hand," he said. "Tell you what. I'll help you unpack your stuff and then we'll go and get a pizza."

"I don't want to."

"Okay, we'll get a curry."

"I don't want to unpack. I don't want to stay here. I want to go home."

Dad let out this long sigh, like he'd been holding his breath all day. He said, "I'm sorry, Tom." The way he said it, I knew there was no point in fighting any more.

I let Dad open the biggest box and start
unpacking my football mags and posters. He
made my bed while I put my clothes away. My
chest of drawers looked bigger in the new room.
After that, I wanted to stop, but Dad made me set
up my computer and music system as well.

"Now can we go and get a pizza?" I said. I just
wanted to get out of that house for a while.
Sid was sitting on the landing looking cross.
His head was down, and his green eyes were
glittering like glass in his dark orange face. The
paler stripes on his back seemed to be bristling
with annoyance. Some people think cats don't
have proper feelings, but Sid definitely does.
We got him years ago, when I was in
playgroup and Mum was still a nurse
She went off him at about the same
time as she went off her job.
She said he had a bad attitude.

"We're going to have to
keep Sid in for a few
weeks," Dad said. "If he
gets out, he'll just go
back to the old house."
I knew how he felt.
"Poor old Sid,"
I said.

Dad picked up his car keys.

"Don't worry. He'll get used to it. It'll just take some time."

We went into town. It had always been a special treat, Dad and me going out on our own, but suddenly it wasn't special any more. Now, this was our normal life, just him and me doing things together. I tried to pretend it still felt great, but we both knew it didn't. We didn't stay long, just had our pizzas and left. Then there wasn't really anything else to do, so we went back to the house. It was getting dark.

Some of the houses in Miller's Row had their
lights on. There was a street light right outside
our place. Propped up against it was a bunch of
yellow flowers. They looked gaudy and bright in
the gloom.

There was no card on them, and no clue how
they got there. I frowned.

"When you see flowers in the street on the
news it means someone has died," I said to Dad.
But he was busy looking for his key and he didn't
seem to hear me.

2 Is Anyone There?

We watched TV till nearly midnight. Sid wouldn't come into the living room. He just sat in the kitchen staring at the back door as if it might fly open by magic if he looked at it for long enough. But I couldn't face going to bed in that cold new bedroom on my own, so I scooped him up and took him with me.

I sat up reading my football mags. Sid jumped onto the windowsill. There weren't any curtains yet so the window looked like a gaping black hole. I could see that Sid was depressed. Normally, he would be outside by now, hunting in the hedges, meeting up with his mates. I got up and gave him a stroke, but he didn't even seem to notice. He just sat staring out at the darkness.

I turned off the light and got back into bed. Now the window seemed suddenly pale. Sid was a black silhouette against the slate-grey sky. I called him, but he just stood up and shifted across to the other end of the windowsill.

As my eyes got used to the dark, I could make out the shapes of my desk and chair, my chest of drawers, and the stool with my bedside light and magazines on it. I closed my eyes.

Everything felt wrong. The room smelled cold. A house should smell of lots of things, like shower gel and toast and warm skin and hot chocolate, but this one didn't smell of anything. It didn't sound right, either. It was too quiet. I missed the hum of the bypass outside, and Mr O'Neil calling his dog to come in. Every movement Dad made

sounded too loud in the silence, Even my own
breathing sounded too loud. It was keeping me
awake. I opened my eyes. The door was in the
wrong place; the window was wrong, all
wrong ...

I didn't think I would ever get to sleep, but I
must have done, because in the middle of the
night something woke me up. I lay still. I felt
frightened because I didn't know what
had woken me. Could there be
burglars downstairs? I turned
my head very slightly so that
I could see the window. It
was just a pale square in
the dark wall. Something
was missing. Sid! I
breathed a sigh of relief.
It must just have been
Sid who woke me by
jumping down off the
windowsill or prowling
around.

Perhaps he had been
scratching at the door to
get out. That was the sort
of thing he did that used to
drive Mum mad.

"Sid," I said, softly. He didn't come. I closed my eyes, and drifted back to sleep.

Something woke me up again. Perhaps Mum had a point. "Sid!" I said. "Cut it out!" He hadn't gone back onto the windowsill. As I looked, I seemed to see curtains swaying across it, gauzy and light. They seemed to be lifting in a breeze, as if the window had been left open. I thought I could feel the breeze on my face.

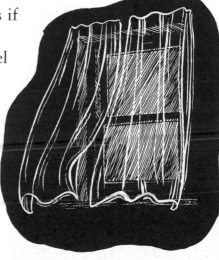

I drifted in and out of sleep like the curtains drifting on the air. Sometimes I knew I was awake, and sometimes I seemed to be dreaming. But the dream was very strange, because it all happened inside my room, as if I were awake.

In the dream, the room was full of furniture. There was my desk and chair, my chest of drawers, but also, like a mark on tracing paper placed in front of them, a big blue cupboard I had never seen before and a wicker chair. I could hear doors slamming downstairs, and I called out, "Is anyone there?"

The door opened, like a tracing paper door in front of the real one, and a boy came into the room. He was older than me and he had a sort of swagger. He didn't seem to notice me at all. He put his skateboard in the gap between the blue cupboard and the wall. He took off his trainers, opened the cupboard and chucked them in. They didn't make any sound.

There was something wrong with this dream. I thought, "It isn't a dream; I'm awake."

Then I thought, "If I'm awake,I'm mad!"
It seemed important that I should find Sid. If he
was here in the room, then I must be awake. No,
that didn't follow ...

The boy shut the cupboard and sat down on
the chair. For a moment, I saw his face more
clearly. He had a big gash on the side of his head,
and dark blood was oozing out of it, running
down his neck. Almost as soon as he sat down, he
started to disappear. He seemed to melt into the

wicker chair. He
seemed to pour
through it like water. Then
the chair melted too. It was sucked away to
wherever the boy went, and the cupboard and the
curtains and the skateboard, all poured away like
water into an invisible plughole.

For a while, I lay stock still in the darkness.
I tried to sit up, but I couldn't move. I couldn't tell
if my eyes were open or closed. I wanted Sid, or
Dad, but I couldn't call out.

I must have gone to sleep because the next

thing I knew, the morning sun streaming through
the window woke me up.
Sid was sitting by the door
looking at me impatiently.
He had already done his
best to let himself
out, judging by the
scratch marks, but
instead of looking
sheepish about the
damage he looked
peevish about the delay.

Mum had a point about his attitude, I thought,
as I followed him downstairs.

3 The Flowers on the Pavement

Dad was sitting on a kitchen chair outside the back door, eating his cornflakes. There was an empty chair beside him.

"Watch you don't let the cat out," he said, catching sight of me through the glass. I dodged past Sid and went out into the garden.

There were eight uneven paving slabs outside the back door with tufts of grass growing up between them. Ants swarmed all over them in the sunshine.

"Did you sleep all right?" Dad asked.

I told him no; I had just spent the worst night of my life. He looked at me and nodded. He wasn't pretending everything was fine any more. "Me too," he said.

There was a furious burst of scratching from behind the kitchen door. "Sid three," I joked. Dad managed a smile.

I wanted to eat my breakfast inside because of the ants. There wasn't much food in the house, so I just had some bread and jam. Dad came in to write a shopping list because he was planning to go to the supermarket while I was at the park. I always played football with my mates on a Sunday morning.

I didn't feel like playing football, but I didn't want to sit around on my own either. When I left the house, the yellow flowers were still there, propped up against the lamp post. They looked more ordinary in the daytime. They were a bit

wilted, and the cellophane round them was torn.
When I got to the end of the road I could see the
park. Miller's Row was closer to the park than the
old house had been, and for the first time, I felt
my spirits lift. It wasn't all bad after all ...

That lasted about one millisecond. Who was I
kidding? It was all terrible. I was living in a
nightmare and I just wanted to get out. I broke
into a run.

There were
usually enough of us
to play five-a-side, but
Luke had gone to his dad's for the
weekend. Otherwise, you would have thought
it was a normal Sunday morning. No one said
anything about me moving, though they all knew.
It was embarrassing. I wanted to show them I was

okay about it, so at half time I said, "My new house is much nearer the park." Then they asked me stuff like did I have a garden and how big was my room, and it started to feel less weird.

After the second half most people had to go straight home because of Sunday lunch. Toad-in-the-hole and roast potatoes was my favourite – but I didn't know when I'd be having that again. I walked back with Sam because Miller's Row was on his way home.

"Which one's your house?" he asked, as we turned the corner.

"The one with the flowers outside."

Sam stopped in his tracks and looked at me.

"You live in the skateboard kid's house?" he exclaimed.

Images from my dream flicked through my mind like pictures on an overhead projector. I felt suddenly sick.

"What skateboard kid?"

I didn't really want to know, but I couldn't help myself.

"The one who got run over by the drunk driver. It was in all the papers."

Sam saw an empty burger box in the gutter,

flicked it up onto the pavement with his toe and started dribbling it along the road. I went after him.

"I was getting a skateboard for Christmas," he told me, doing a neat back kick. "Then my mum goes and reads about this stupid accident and decides I can't have one any more. Skateboarding is too dangerous she says."

We came to the flowers and stopped.

"Bit droopy, aren't they?" said Sam. "That skateboard kid, what was his name now?"

Sam looked up at the sky as if he expected the name to fall out of it.

"Got it!" he said. "His name was Ryan Grey!"

4 My Sister, the Goth

Dad was home from the supermarket and the chips were in the oven. He and Sid weren't talking to each other because Sid had trashed the living room while we were both out. I was thinking about the skateboard boy and it was doing my head in. Wasn't it a bit of a coincidence that I dreamed about someone who had lived in the house … someone who had died right outside it?

"Mel's coming round later," Dad said. Like that was supposed to cheer me up.

"Okay," I shrugged.

Most of the time I thought Mel was a total pain. Just because she was older than me, she thought she was really big. She hung out with a bunch of weirdos, and at weekends she was a goth (she couldn't be a goth at school because it didn't exactly fit with the uniform rules).

What was the point of putting on pale face

make-up and wearing black lipstick? I didn't get it. Also, why would anyone want to spend three hours clogging up the bathroom trying to get their hair to look as if it had all fallen out and been stuck back on in random handfuls? Who would go out and buy perfectly good clothes and then tear great big holes in them the minute they got them home? And did anyone actually need a stud in their bottom lip?

Mel and her mates used to be round our house the whole time, playing music by *Pus* and *The Ravenous Rats*, only it wasn't so much music as yelling and screeching, and you really didn't want to listen to the words. There were always rows

about the noise, and Dad would end up going ballistic. "I can't take much more of this!" he would shout. Well, now he didn't have to, and it seemed to me that maybe all that goth stuff was what drove my mum and dad apart.

Mel hadn't seemed that bothered when they told us they were splitting up. She'd just shrugged and said okay, as if they'd said they were going to the shops or something.

"Is that it?" I'd snapped at her. "Is that all you can say?"

I'd wanted to hit her, but then Dad had said, "At least it means you two won't have to live under the same roof any more," and I thought, "Is it our fault then? Are they breaking up the family because Mel and I don't get on?"

We didn't talk about it after that. It seemed like there was nothing left to say, or maybe there was too much and you could never say it all. I knew Mel wouldn't want to go and live with Dad so it made sense for me to. You can't just abandon your parents; you have responsibilities. I didn't want to lose either of them, but at least this way we all still had someone.

Dad cleared the dishes and we watched the football for a while, eating mini doughnuts from the bag. The match was just getting interesting

when Mel arrived and Dad turned it off. He
would never have done that in the old house, in
the old life.

Mel looked a nightmare in black as usual, but
at least she hadn't brought any of her goth friends
with her. She flopped down on the sofa and
helped herself to a doughnut.

"How's the flat?" Dad said.

"Small. Could be worse. How's the house?"

"Ditto."

"You gonna show me round, then?"

"If you've got five seconds to spare."

They seemed to be getting on fine so I left them
to it and switched the TV back on. When they
had finished looking round, they came back in
and Dad turned it off again. It seemed like he
wanted me to say something

"What do you think?" I asked Mel.

Not that I wanted to hear it.

"Garden's a bit rubbish, but at least you've got one," she said. "We've only got a concrete parking space in the alley behind the flats."

She took the last doughnut.

"Kitchen's okay I suppose. This room's a bit pokey. Dad's bedroom's okay and the bathroom's okay. What colour are you going to paint your room?"

I hadn't thought about it.

"Only it feels a bit chilly, doesn't it, with all that white? But it's okay, I suppose."

Dad got some bottles of cola and we went outside. Mel wasn't bothered about the ants; goths can't be feeble. In the sunshine, you could see that her face was a bit puffy under the pale make-up, and her eyes looked red as if she had been crying.

"What?" she demanded, seeing me looking at her.

Usually, when Mel says "What?" like that, you duck. But it was like all the stuffing had gone out of her; she was all mouth and no muscle. I nearly felt sorry for her.

I went to have a poke around in the shed. The door was hanging by one hinge. When I tried to pull it open it fell off. Inside, ivy was growing

down through the roof and there were big holes in
the sides. There was an old mattress leaning
against the wall at the back. I looked behind it
and found a dead mouse, all shrivelled up. There
wouldn't be mice around the place once Sid was
on the loose, I thought.

I started looking through some boxes of stuff
on the floor. You never knew what you might find
in an old shed like that. I was on the second box
when I heard a crash in the kitchen, and saw Dad
running back inside, swearing about the cat. Mel
came down the garden.

"I'm going now," she said.

"Right. Bye, then."

I went on sifting through the box.

"I forgot to tell you," she said. "Mum says 'Hi'."

She went on standing there, I went on sifting.

"When are you going to come and see the flat?"

"Sometime."

"I'm painting my room black."

"You don't say."

Why wasn't she going? I came out of the shed.

"Did you want something?" I said.

"Only Mum and Dad to get back together." Her voice was thin, as if she could only squeeze a little bit out.

"Maybe you should've thought of that before," I said.

She gave me this really odd look.

"It's pretty bad already," she said. "Do we have to make it worse?"

5 The Ghost of Ryan Grey

I couldn't sleep again. I read my mags, turned the light off, tried to go to sleep, turned the light on again, read my mags … Sid was downstairs in the living room. Knocking the dirty dishes off the kitchen surface seemed to have been his last attempt at making us give in and let him out. After that he had gone into a sulk. He was sitting in the corner behind the armchair, looking at the wall.

I lay in bed in the dark, not wanting to close my eyes. The light from the hall made a yellow rectangle around the door. I had pinned my England banner over the window to make it look less stark. I heard Dad come upstairs.

THE GHOST OF RYAN GREY

He turned the hall light off and closed his
bedroom door behind him. I could hear him
moving about.

It was cold in my room, and there seemed to be
a draught coming from the window. I got out of
bed to check that it was shut properly. Suddenly,
the banner billowed out as if a gust of wind had
hit it, and I jumped back onto my bed. The
banner looked thin and gauzy like a curtain now. I
couldn't take my eyes off it.

There was a shift in the air, some things
slipping away, other things pushing forward. I
could see the blue cupboard out of the corner of
my eye, emerging through the wall like a blue box
surfacing through water. The wicker chair was
firming up, from a faint outline to a flat image,
and then fully into three dimensions, right before
my eyes. The door flew open and I spun round.

He put the skateboard in the gap between the
cupboard and the wall. I shut my eyes tight and
then opened them again. He was still there. He
undid the laces of his trainers. At any time, he
might look up and see me. I sat stock still, hardly
daring to breathe.

The boy threw his trainers into the cupboard.
They didn't make a sound. He shut the cupboard
door. Then he went to sit on the chair. I could see

the livid gash on the side of his head, and the trickle of dark red blood.

He was only there for a few seconds and then, as suddenly as he had come, he disappeared. He melted into the chair, and the chair melted after him, and then the blue cupboard. They were all sucked away like water down an invisible plughole.

For a long time, I couldn't move. I just sat bolt upright on my bed as still as a statue, but my head was spinning with crazy thoughts. I knew I was awake … or did I? I thought I was awake. Well, I hadn't been to sleep. Or had I? I tried to remember if at any time I might have dozed off over my magazine.

If I hadn't been asleep, and the boy really had come into the room, well that meant ... what did it mean?

It wasn't possible. It simply could not have been the way it seemed.

Perhaps I imagined the blue cupboard. Something in the room, a pattern of shadows on the wall, for instance, maybe just looked like a cupboard. Once, when I was little, I thought my dressing gown hanging on the back of the door at night was a monster. But there was nothing in this room that suggested a big blue cupboard.

My gaze came to rest on the door. I frowned. Earlier on, before Dad went to bed, the hall light had made a perfect rectangle around it because it was shut. The hall beyond was dark now and the door glimmered palely in the faint light from the window. It was not shut any more.

My heart was pounding. I couldn't take my eyes off the door. I wanted Dad, but I couldn't go out into the hall. I reached out to turn on my bedside light, but my hand was shaking so much that I couldn't find the switch. Come on! Come on! At last, I found the switch, but as I fumbled to turn it on the light tipped away over the far edge of the stool and went crashing down onto the floor.

There was a noise that might have been me crying out, and then the door flew open ...

6 In the Dark

"What happened?"

Dad came over to the bed and sat down.

"I d-don't know."

My voice was shaking as much as the rest of me. Dad picked up the bedside light and put it back on the stool. He switched it on. I blinked, in the sudden brightness.

"You look as if you've seen a ghost!" he remarked.

"I h-have. I have seen a g-ghost. It was the skateboard boy!"

Dad frowned. He didn't ask who the skateboard boy was. He knew about the skateboard boy! He had known all along, but he hadn't told me.

"You knew why the flowers were outside the house," I said. "Why didn't you tell me about the skateboard boy?"

"Because I thought you'd just get upset. I thought you might have nightmares, or start imagining things."

He gave me a steady look, a look that said quite plainly, "And I was right, wasn't I? You are imagining things ..."

"I didn't imagine it. He was here."

Dad said ghosts didn't really exist; they were figments of your imagination. He said I must have heard about the skateboard boy and that started me thinking about him. I had built up such a good mental picture of him that in my half-asleep state I had imagined I could actually see him.

"But the first time I saw him I didn't know about him at all," I said. "Sam told me afterwards."

"You must have known. You probably just forgot that you knew. You might have read about what happened in the newspapers months ago,

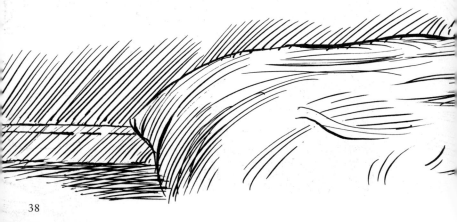

and then it slipped your mind. Anyway, there's no such thing as ghosts."

Dad said that as he wasn't sleeping very well either, we might as well sit up for a while. We took our quilts and went downstairs. Dad went out into the kitchen to make some hot chocolate and toast. I curled up on the sofa. From time to time, Sid glared out at me from under the chair.

There was an old gangster film on, but we weren't really watching it. Dad kept trying to

make me feel better, by saying things like,
"Sometimes the mind plays tricks," and "You're
bound to be feeling unsettled."

"It's not easy for any of us," he said.

"Then why are we doing it? Why don't we just
go home?"

"You know why we're doing it," Dad said.
"Things weren't working out."

"Things seemed okay to me. Nobody told me
anything. Like you didn't tell me about the
skateboard boy. You just left me in the dark."

I pushed the rest of my toast away. I didn't
want it any more.

"If I'd known, I could've tried not to argue
with Mel so much. I could've made her stop being
such a pain …"

Dad looked surprised. "It wasn't anything to
do with you and Mel," he said.

"Then what was it?" I asked. "You and Mum
didn't even have rows. Why would you want to
split up?"

He shrugged. "When you first get married, you
have a sort of dream about the future. You have
the same dream. Well, Mum and me, we've been
drifting apart for a while. We want to go in
different directions now, because we're not
sharing the same dream any more."

"But what about Mel and me? Don't we get any say in it?"

"Mum and I will always be there for both of you. Always. That's why we've decided to live really close to each other while you're growing up, so that you will be able to come and go whenever you like."

The gangsters had walked into the trap and now the cops were going to kill them. It was all in black and white, so it didn't look real. When they fell down, black blood poured out of them.

Dad said, "Why don't you go and see Mum and Mel in the morning? I'm sure it'll make you feel better."

"Like putting a plaster on the bullet holes would stop all that black blood," I thought. Who was he kidding? I didn't bother to answer him. I still felt angry about it all, but at least we had talked about it now, and by some miracle, I still hadn't blubbed. But I didn't know how I would handle seeing Mum.

7 Talking to Mel

I could have taken the bus, but I decided to walk.
Dad and I had dozed all night on the
sofa and I was still feeling fuzzy and
half asleep. The flowers had fallen over
and someone had cycled over them. I
wondered what the skateboard boy
would think of some kid cycling over
his flowers. I wondered who had
left them there for him, and
where they were now.

When I thought about him
I could easily picture him
walking into my room, putting
his skateboard away, throwing his
trainers into the cupboard. Perhaps Dad was right,
and he was just a figment of my imagination. But I
wasn't going to sleep in that bedroom again, that
was for sure. I would sleep in the kitchen, the

bathroom, the garden – I would sleep anywhere, but not in the skateboard boy's room.

Mum's flat was on the ground floor of a big old house in Albert Street. It had a tidy patch of grass in front and a brick path up to the door. There were three doorbells and each one had a name card above it. I didn't want to ring the bell, but my hand seemed to have ideas of its own. Before I had a chance to change my mind Mum came to the door.

Mum was a great one for hugging, but I didn't want her to hug me now, and she didn't. She's also a great one for picking up signals.

She showed me around. At the front, there was a big sitting room with a wide window. The hall had a tiled floor, which made our footsteps sound loud. Mum had the biggest bedroom and Mel had the second biggest, but we couldn't go in because she was painting behind the door. There was one more small room with nothing in it. Mum said she was going to put a bed in there for me, so that I could stay over any time I liked.

She didn't ask me how things were going in Miller's Row and I didn't tell her. I didn't really want to talk, but just to get this first visit over and done with. As it happened, she had to go into the office for a few hours anyway.

"Make yourself a milk shake," she said, "and have a dig around in the kitchen for something to eat. Mel won't be long."

I thought it was a bit off, her going to work so soon after I had arrived. I would have thought Dad would have told her that I was coming, so she could fix up to be at home. That's the kind of thing they used to do before, but maybe they weren't talking any more, even about Mel and me. Maybe they would never talk again.

There was a choice of strawberry or banana, which was good because I knew Mum had got the banana for me – no one else liked it. I cut myself a chunk of bread and a slice of fruit cake that had already been opened. Mum and Mel would never get through a whole fruit cake on their own and I was happy to help them out!

Digging around in the cupboards and finding stuff to eat was good. It meant I didn't feel like a visitor any more, but like someone who belonged.

I went into the living room and put the radio on. Mel's CD cases were scattered all over the place. One of them had a vampire on the  front. One had a graveyard with a red ghoul coming up out of a grave. The skateboard boy hadn't looked weird and creepy; he was just like a normal kid, but without the noise. Perhaps that meant he couldn't be a ghost.

There was a crash, which was probably Mel jumping down off a chair in her big boots. Mel pushed the door open. If someone had been there with a camera, it would've made a great cover for one of her CDs. Her face was white, her eyes looked as if they were melting into black puddles and her mouth was dark purple inside a black line. She was wearing an assortment of clothes in several shades of black, which made her look like the leftovers table at a jumble sale. She was holding a paintbrush in one hand like a dagger, and black paint was splattered half way up her arms.

"It's finished!" she announced. "Well, the first coat, anyway. Come and see."

Her room was a complete mess.

All her stuff was piled up in the middle of the floor, and her bed was tipped on its side with the bedding falling off. The walls were black. She hadn't done the edges very well, so there was black paint creeping up onto the ceiling and down over the carpet too.

"What do you think?"

"Well, I guess it won't show the dirt," I said. She laughed. She had a new laugh she was trying out. I think she was going for devilish, which was an improvement on the old witch's cackle. She got cleaned up and made herself a sandwich. She actually seemed glad that I was there, and I realised it must be just as odd for her being on her own with Mum all the time as it was for me being with Dad.

"I can't do a second coat until that one's dry,"
she said. "D'you wanna watch a video?"

"What've you got?"

She dug out half a dozen horror movies from
the heap in her bedroom. "This one might be
okay," she said. It was called *The Haunting of
Hangcliffe House*.

"Do you believe in all that sort of stuff?" I
said. "You know – ghosts?"

"Of course I do."

"Dad says they're a figment of the imagination."

"Dad hasn't got any imagination."

She gave a devilish laugh. I wouldn't normally

talk to Mel about things, but there was nothing normal about this day.

"I've seen a ghost."

Mel looked at me to check if I was lying.

"Where?"

"In the new house. In my room."

I told her about the skateboard boy. I said I wasn't going to sleep in his room any more. She nodded, as if she suddenly understood.

"So that's what this is all about! You want to come and live here."

"No! That's not it. I really have seen a ghost. I thought you might know how to get rid of it."

Mel took a deep breath and blew it out through her teeth. She was thinking. She said, "You need an exorcist. I've seen it in a film. The exorcist comes and chucks holy water about, and makes a spell or something."

"Do you know one?"

"No. But anyway, what would Dad think? You'd have to run it past him first."

"So what am I going to do?"

Mel put *The Haunting of Hangcliffe House* in the machine. "This might give us some ideas," she said. "But if it doesn't, I'll ask Doomus. He'll know."

Doomus was one of Mel's mad mates. He had a nail through one of his ears, a proper nail he'd put in with a hammer, and he was famous for doing his own tattoos. If there weren't any hints in *The Haunting of Hangcliffe House* it looked like I was pretty well sunk.

8 Ice in the Bones

"How was Mum?"

"Okay. She had to go to work."

"Was that all right?"

"Yes."

I suddenly wondered if Dad had been in touch with Mum after all, to tell her I was going. Maybe they had actually set it up so that she would go out because then I'd have to make myself at home.

"How's Mel?"

"She's painted her room black."

"Nice! Want to see what I've been doing?"

I followed Dad out the back. Sid wasn't in the kitchen; he was still in a sulk.

Dad had cleared all the nettles and brambles from the garden and heaped them up near the paved area by the back door. He had pulled down the shed and cleared away the rubbish that was inside it. Now the garden looked wider, and you

could see the whole path with areas of brown earth on either side. The high wall at the bottom was completely bare. Dad said he had great plans for our little garden. I tried to humour him.

"It's looking much better now," I lied. Like it was ever going to be a touch on our old garden with its trees and grass and my football goal.

We had spaghetti for tea; pasta's about the only thing Dad can cook that doesn't come out of a box (though his sauce does come out of a jar).

I didn't mention until bedtime that I wasn't going to bed, and Dad didn't take it too well. He said I was being silly with all this talk about ghosts.

"How long are you going to keep this up?" Dad said. As if it was some kind of game.

I couldn't blame him for not taking me seriously. After all, I hadn't believed in ghosts either until I had actually seen one. Also, I knew he wasn't going to back down. So I decided to go up and wait until he went to bed, then creep back downstairs and sleep on the sofa.

I didn't like being in the room. I didn't want to get into bed because that's where I had been when I saw him. But if he came when I was at my desk, how would that work? Would I be swallowed up like my desk and chair as his furniture came through into the room from wherever it was right now?

I sat on the windowsill. I could hear the TV downstairs. A programme was finishing. I hoped Dad would turn it off and come upstairs, but then a new programme started and I knew it would be at least another half an hour before he came. Half an hour! A lot could happen in half an hour. Did I feel a slight draught from the window behind me? Was there a smudge of blue on the wall? Or was it just my mind playing tricks?

The sharp sound of my mobile phone ringing on the bedside table made me jump. I picked it up. It was Mel. At eleven o'clock?

"Mel?"

"I've found out something. Doomus told me. He said sometimes ghosts are just confused. He said if a person dies suddenly they might not realise they're dead. They don't know they've got to move on, so they just keep coming back. They don't know they shouldn't be here any more. Someone has to tell them."

"Who has to tell them?"

"Anyone. You can do it yourself."

"Are you kidding?"

"What choice have you got?"

If she had been in the house at that moment, I might have grovelled. Even though we didn't get on that well, I could still play the little brother card sometimes, and get her to do things for me. There must be some kind of big sister instinct that kicks in. But she wasn't in the house; she was in a flat in Albert Street, and I was all on my own.

"Tom? Are you still there?"

"Yes. I was thinking."

"He might not come back anyway."

"N-no. I suppose not."

"Text me later if you want. I'll leave my phone on."

I sat on my bed. My brain felt numb. I didn't notice the time passing, but it must've done because I suddenly realised that the TV was off, and I could hear Dad in his bedroom getting ready for bed. I picked up my quilt and went to the door. The landing light was off. I tiptoed downstairs.

Sid looked up when I went into the living room, but he didn't bother to move. I went to stroke him; he turned his head away.

I was beginning to feel fed up with him. "It's already bad. Do we have to make it worse?"

That's what Mel had said to me. That's what I wanted to say to Sid.

I couldn't put the TV on because Dad might hear. I sat on the sofa under my quilt. I thought about the skateboard boy. What was the house like when he lived in it? Did he have a mum and a dad? Sisters and brothers? Did he have a temperamental pet? If he did, they were gone now. All gone. How must it be for him, to keep coming back and finding everything he had was gone?

The skateboard boy wasn't scary like the red ghoul on Mel's CD, he was just a kid. If he was alive I wouldn't be frightened of him. He hadn't done anything to harm me. He hadn't even noticed me, now I came to think about it. If it was me coming back to a house I didn't belong in any more – say, going back to my old house, for example – and everyone was gone, and all my things were gone, and there were new people living there ... If it was me, I would want someone to explain things to me. I would want someone to say, "You don't belong here now. You have to move on."

I went upstairs. My bedside light was still on. I sat on the bed and waited. Nothing happened. I was shivering so I put on a sweater, but I still couldn't stop.

I felt it coming before I saw anything. A stream of cold air blew across from the window, and the

gauzy curtains lifted in on it. The blue cupboard
floated up through the wall. The wicker chair. The
door opened and the skateboard boy came in. He
put his skateboard in the gap between the
cupboard and the wall. He took off his trainers
and threw them into the cupboard. They didn't
make a sound. I tried to say something, but my
voice stuck in my throat. Then the skateboard boy
went towards the wicker chair …

I only had a few seconds now. I knew that as
soon as he sat down he would begin to fade, and I
would lose my chance. But if he saw me, if he
heard me, what would happen then? I couldn't

think about that. I had to think about him, coming back to a house where there was nothing for him any more, and me, trying to move into a space that still belonged to someone else.

"Hello."

He turned towards me. He was looking at me, but he wasn't seeing me. He was listening, like you do if you think you hear someone calling from far, far away, but you aren't sure where they are. I felt cold trickling through my whole body, like ice in the bones.

"I'm Tom."

He didn't move for several seconds, and then he seemed to hear what I said, and he frowned. I said, "You can't stay here now, Ryan Grey. You've got to move on."

Once more, it seemed to take several seconds for my words to reach him, although we were only a few feet apart. But how can you measure the distance between the living and the dead?

The skateboard boy stared at me more intently than ever. I didn't know if he could see me.

I said, "You're dead. You were knocked down

by a car. You don't belong here any more. I'm sorry."

He moved, and I thought he was going to come towards me. I caught my breath. Then he turned away, and as he turned, the blue cupboard and the wicker chair suddenly dissolved into the air. The skateboard boy walked straight towards the wall. He melted through it.

I couldn't move. I couldn't breathe. But I couldn't stay in that room either. With my heart pounding in my ears, I forced myself up off the bed and raced out of the door. I ran back downstairs, dived under the quilt and shut my eyes tight.

9 Breathing Again

When the phone rang I thought it was an alarm clock. But then I heard Dad come into the living room and pick it up. I drifted in and out of sleep, hearing little bits of conversation, wondering vaguely who he was talking to.

"... You don't say! ... He slept downstairs again ... That's a good idea ..."

I sat up and rubbed my eyes.

Dad was off the phone now, and he had gone into the kitchen to make some breakfast.

"Who was that?" I asked.

"Mum. She says Mel wants to dye all her bedding black, and get some black curtains!" He came in with two mugs of tea.

"Mum reckons it might be a good idea if we started sorting your room out today. What do you think?"

I nodded, but I didn't say anything.

After breakfast, we went up to my room to measure the windows and think about what colour scheme would be best.

The sun was streaming in through the window and, for the first time, the room felt warm. Sid was curled up asleep on the bed.

I wanted a bright colour for the walls. Then I would have one whole wall full of footballers, and a pin board for school stuff over my desk. I could see it all now, how I wanted it to be, because suddenly it felt like my room and not the skateboard boy's.

We went to the trading estate on the ring road and bought some paint in *Warm Yellow*. We got window blinds instead of curtains because they looked really cool. While Dad was paying I sent Mel a text: "I told him and he's gone. Thanx." Then we went to the garden centre and Dad ordered some stuff.

That afternoon, I heaped all my things up in the middle of the room like Mel had done. I cleared the walls and started to paint. Dad offered to help but I didn't want him to, and he said that was great because there were other things he could be getting on with.

I didn't make such a mess of it as Mel. Not much went over the ceiling and floor. When I got to the window, I stopped. Dad was out in the garden with a man I didn't know.

Somehow, the whole of the far end was green! How could grass grow so quickly, in a couple of hours?

While I watched, Dad and the man laid a roll of turf at the edge of the grass and unrolled it just as if they were laying a carpet. By the time I had finished painting my room, our garden was covered with lawn, except the paved area and the path.

By the end of the day we were worn out. We ordered some takeaway. While we were waiting for it to arrive, Dad put the picnic table outside on the paved area. It was a warm, still evening. I had a bottle of cola and he had a beer, and he talked about how he was going to get some big tubs with trees in and some hanging baskets, and

then we'd have flowers in the garden as well, and it'd look great.

We sat outside for ages. When it started to get dark Dad lit a candle and we played cards by candlelight. Sid sat at the kitchen window looking out, like a poor little prisoner.

I didn't sleep in my own room that night because of the smell of paint, and the next day I did a second coat so I still couldn't sleep in there. It was Saturday night before I slept in my own room again. I took Sid with me, but not because I was scared this time – just because he looked so fed up. He didn't go to the window at all, but curled up by my feet and went to sleep.

Luke was back from visiting his dad so we played five-a-side football the next day. He lived in the middle of town, so we walked back together because I was having dinner at Mum's – toad-in-the-hole. Mel said next time Dad and I had takeaway, she would be coming over to ours.

Mel wanted to know all about what happened with the skateboard boy. I told her. She didn't think I was making it all up and she didn't laugh at me. When I had finished, she said, "You've got some guts, little bro'!" which was quite a compliment, coming from her.

When I left, Mum gave me a hug. Suddenly, it was really hard to go. I took the bus back to Miller's Row. A few hours before, I had felt happy, knowing I could come and go, being with Dad, being with Mum, talking to Mel instead of arguing with her all the time, but now it all felt too hard and too complicated. I didn't know if I could

manage it. I let myself back into the house quietly
and went up to my room.

When I started to cry it was frightening, I had
so many tears. They just kept coming, pouring
down, they wouldn't stop. They wore me out, all
those tears, and I fell asleep.

I woke up because Dad was calling me. I
noticed straight away that I felt different. Before
I'd felt as if I my chest had been wrapped in tight
bandages, and now they had gone – and I hadn't
fallen apart. I was breathing again.

I went to the window. Dad was standing
outside looking up.

"What do you think?" he said, pointing towards the bottom of the garden.

In the middle of the high wall, Dad had painted a goal.

"Come and have a kick around!" he said.

Sid followed me downstairs. He stood by the kitchen door while I put my trainers on.

Dad opened the door and Sid went bounding out. I tried to stop him.

"Don't worry," said Dad. "I think he's settled in now. Who's going in goal?"